Adrian at LARGE

Adrian at LARGE

MARIO HERBERT

CONTENTS

Shaken 1

The Heist 21

New Clothes 39

SHAKEN

The sun was beating down on a desolate school yard like the heat of an oven on a browning loaf. Its rays were unimpeded by clouds and its heat defied the wind which blew falling leaves across an eroding driveway. The peace and quiet of that afternoon was only temporary, however, and that was soon proven. The silence was suddenly scattered by the piercing sound of an electronic bell. Coupled with that sound was the roar of a thousand voices and the boom of two thousand feet.

Adrian stepped out of his classroom, almost in a panic. He was still trying to make a crucial decision—try to board the popular bus or board the unpopular one he usually took.

"It won't be easy to get a seat in the popular bus," he thought to himself, "but all of the popular children will be in it, and I so need to change my image."

He was suddenly snapped back into the present by the realisation that the stampede of his peers was almost upon him. He knew that he had to make a decision quickly. He looked around and saw a multitude of children rushing towards him and the decision was made. Some had already passed him and he couldn't afford to let the others catch him. He started moving, fuelled by anxiety and driven by determination.

"I have to get into that bus," he thought as he ran.

He reached the driveway and could see his target parked just beyond the gate. It glistened brightly in the intense sun and was adorned with spoilers and other accessories. There were children already inside.

"How did they get down here so quickly?" he wondered.

His sense of wonder was soon multiplied as he realised the stampede had reached him. He tried to increase his pace but the bag on his back felt as though it was increasing in weight by the second. Also, he had to be careful not to trip in any potholes as the driveway was in a state of gross disrepair.

Suddenly, a girl who was running next to him tripped and stumbled. She tried to steady herself but she was moving too quickly. As Adrian continued to run, he could see her falling forward, failing to regain stability. He could feel her pain as her body connected with the worn pavement. He could feel her humiliation as she rolled slightly down the drive. Then he was aghast at the fact that the footsteps behind him did not stop.

"Oh my gosh, they're trampling her!" he thought.

His compassion was short-lived, however, as his eyes fell on the bus again. He was almost there; he just had to keep his pace, and stability.

Finally, he reached the bus but found he was unable to access the vehicle. The doorway was inundated with children. He tried to push but did not possess the strength to propel himself through the crowd. Wedged between a rock and a smelly place, he glanced to the right and noticed a few of the bigger children climbing through windows.

"Oh no," he thought, "I'll never get a seat!"

As the crowd continued to push, Adrian found that he was serendipitously shuttled through the door, by little action on his part. Finally inside the bus, he made a joyous discovery; there was a vacant seat. He knew the chances of getting a seat were infinitesimal at best, and had given up hope, but things had changed. He saw a fifth-former about to climb through a window and he rushed into the vacant seat.

The inside of the bus was painted in bright colours with intricate airbrushed artwork. There was a fully airbrushed plaque behind each seat. They served not only to hide the roughness of the underlying upholstery, but they also displayed the name ascribed unto the bus. Adrian found the artwork quite engaging but the name of the bus sent a shudder down his spine. The name *Turbulence* was airbrushed behind each seat and was even featured in the decorative window tint. He told himself that it was just a name and that the benefits he would derive from the trip would outweigh any "turbulence" encountered.

As the bus became increasingly cramped, Adrian savoured his moment of triumph. He had actually defeated the odds and was seated in the popular bus, with the popular children. He was convinced that all eyes were on him.

"Everyone is seeing me in this bus," he thought, "and they're probably wondering if I am really as uncool as they thought."

He remembered all the times that he had endured ridicule at school, just because he had different interests. Now he had an opportunity to show his peers that he was in tune with the same things they were. He had entered their world and fared better than some of them, for he had a seat while many of the regulars were standing.

Unfortunately, Adrian's triumph was short-lived. An unusually large fifth-former, named Ricardo, boarded the bus and scanned the interior. His flat face was garnished with a nose like that of a hippo, and his head was matted with thick shrubbery. He was not only large, but remarkably dark; his skin resembled a freshly tarred road. He also had pronounced veins in the area of his eyes that is normally white; his had a pinkish cast, with piercing black pupils which eventually made eye contact with Adrian. Ricardo displayed the same smile of triumph Adrian had displayed a few moments ago.

"Move, lil man!" he bellowed.

Adrian dared not disobey. There were no teachers, no principals, and the prefects were off duty. A bewildered and embarrassed Adrian surrendered the seat to Ricardo and tried to fit into the standing crowd, but the huge bag he was carrying proved problematic. It stood out like a camel's hump and agitated others. An impatient conductor commanded Adrian to pass the bag, which was then haphazardly thrown on top of the engine cover with many others.

The engine was positioned at the front of the bus, between the driver and the front passenger. Its cover was doubling as an area for bags to be heaped and as a seat. Popular children who failed to secure a seat were afforded the privilege of sitting on the engine. Adrian was dissatisfied with the treatment of his bag but there was no time to focus on that. He had found himself wedged into the middle of the aisle. There was a boy directly behind him and a girl had stationed herself in front of him, partially standing on his shoes. He tried to look around him but apart from the window in front of him, it was impossible to see outside. The conductor came around at the windows and collected the fare. This was the first time Adrian had a chance to examine the conductor's appearance; he was clear, tall and lanky with unkempt hair. There was a thin line between his shabby, washed-out uniform and a collection of rags. He stood at the window before Adrian, extending his hand for payment. It was difficult for Adrian to access his pockets in this crowd. He managed to squeeze his hand into his pocket and secured his fare, which he had to pass to the conductor via the girl who stood on his shoes. He dared not drop any of it, for he knew that recovery would be impossible. Adrian was displeased with the conditions he was presently subjected to but soon the engine started and he chose to focus on the ride.

After the conductor apologised for the radio being broken, the bus started off with a jolt and the driver held the first gear for what seemed like forever.

"Why is he doing that?" thought Adrian. "Doesn't he know that can destroy the gear box?"

But the children didn't care about the mechanical health of the vehicle, and they raised a loud roar in approval of the driver's actions.

"Hold it, driver, hold it!" they chanted, until the engine started to "stammer", resulting in even louder shouts of approval.

Finally, the driver got down to the business of real driving, suddenly changing the gears and hurtling down the road at mind-boggling speed. Adrian could barely make out where he was. Everything was a blur outside the window.

The children started chanting, "Max it out, driver. Maximum!"

Adrian was white with fear, especially as he couldn't see what was in front of the bus.

"I've gone through all of this to be more popular," he thought, "I might as well look the part."

He resolved to participate in the chanting, fuelled by the prospect of receiving the acceptance he so craved from his peers. Adrian joined the chant and tried to look as though he was accustomed to such recklessness, but nothing could prepare him for what happened next.

The driver geared down and prepared to turn onto a big hill, with many winding bends and parked cars. There were houses on both sides of the hill and many residents were outside in their patios taking in the breeze.

The chant of the children changed to, "Give it to us, driver, give it to us!"

As the bus started up the hill, Adrian was looking through the window before him. He could see the windows of the houses on the right side of the hill. He could also see the patios and the people in them. They were staring wide-eyed at the bus, presumably amazed at the quantity of humans in it. Adrian's mind started to wander. He wondered how many children were really in the bus. From his vantage point it seemed like at least fifty people were standing in the bus, which was only licensed and insured to carry seven standing passengers. This train of thought was interrupted as Adrian noticed a gradual build-up of pressure from behind him. He could feel the weight of the children behind him compressing him.

"What's going on?" he wondered, until he looked through the window and noticed that he was no longer seeing houses but the pavement of the road they were on.

This realisation scared Adrian greatly, but then he noticed the houses were coming back into view, as well as the people in the patios. This time, however, the people in the patios were staring and pointing at the bus with their jaws dropped. As his angle of view continued to change, he could see the tops of the houses and the pressure had eased from behind him. By this time the children were franticly hitting the sides of the bus, not in fear, but in great approval of the driver's antics.

"Shakes. Give us the shakes!" chanted the children, much to Adrian's dismay.

It was at this point that the realisation of what was really going on came to Adrian. The driver was using the sharpness of the winds in the hill, in conjunction with the weight of the children, to rock the bus from side to side. He was even occasionally swerving sharply off the parked cars to rock the bus further. This motion continued up the hill. As Adrian looked through the window he was consistently presented with a view of pavement, then houses, then rooftops, followed by the reverse. They were almost at the top of the hill and the children's chorus continued until Adrian realised that he had been looking at pavement for a longer period of time than previously experienced.

"Oh no, the driver can't get this thing upright again," he thought. "We are going to turn over."

Adrian's fear and alarm were augmented with utter astonishment as the children, seemingly realising that the bus wasn't reverting to the upright position, began a new chant.

"Kill, kill, kill!" they shouted. "Kill us all, driver!"

Adrian had reached the threshold of his compo-sure. He had difficulty breathing and he started to sweat uncontrollably. Everything around him seemed to be intensified. The repugnant odour of the children between whom he was wedged, seemed to be asphyxi-ating him. The lunchtime and after-school sweat of over fifty individuals was all intermingled and seemed to be mangling his nostrils.

"I'm going to die," he thought, while gasping for

breath. "If the crash doesn't kill me the odour will."

He started to see visions of his life's most significant events—birthdays, accomplishments etc., flashing before his eyes.

Suddenly, his visions were interrupted by the wailing of a siren. His anxiety dwindled, but was not extinguished, as the bus finally returned to an upright position and was escorted by a bike-mounted policeman a short distance to the top of the hill. Now halted at the top of the hill, the police officer dismounted his bike and approached the bus.

"Okay, I want seven people standing in this bus," he shouted, "so start filing out until I have that number!"

As the children filed out of the bus, the policeman counted them. By the time Adrian retrieved his bag from the engine and stepped out the door, he heard the policeman count him as number seventy-five. Adrian could not believe that seventy-five children had been standing in the bus, or rather, more, because they were still children exiting and he hadn't included the seven who were permitted by law. He now had opportunity to examine the officer. He was clear, short and frail-looking with a narrow face and a nose like an arrow. Adrian looked at him with great disdain.

"Shouldn't he be out hunting criminals?" Adrian thought, angrily. "This is annoying!"

He comforted himself with the thought that at least it was over, but then a startling realisation hit him like a cold hand; he did not have enough money to catch another bus to get to town. If he did, he wouldn't be able to get home from town, but then he heard a girl speak.

"Follow me. I know some 'back roads' that we can take to intercept the bus further in the route."

Adrian knew the girl only from seeing her; she was not easy to miss. Her hair was stuck together by an excessive amount of hair gel and her uniform hugged her body like a rubber band on a cow's torso. Facially, she was not the prettiest girl in the school but the accentuation of her shape was sufficient compensation for Adrian.

Adrian didn't want to get back in the bus but it was his only chance to get to town. He could also see social benefits, however remote, from following the African goddess who was leading the group. Sharing this experience with her somehow made him feel as though they were close. He started to follow the children through a residential area, all the while, wondering if they could really get back onto the main road before the bus passed.

"Don't worry," said the girl who was leading, as if in prophetic reply to Adrian.

"The officer's going to report the conductor for overloading and the driver for 'shaking', so we' got a little time."

The children ran through residential areas, panting and sweating all the way. Adrian couldn't tell how many of them were trying to re-board the bus. He knew it wasn't all who were put off, but it was still a lot of them.

People were looking at them through windows and

from patios, some shaking their heads with disapproving looks. Adrian felt like a refugee, fleeing through foreign territory with hopes of returning to the place from whence he was exiled. As they ran, they could hear people's dogs barking.

"What if a dog attacks us?" Adrian thought.

"I could be disfigured for life, and when I get out of the hospital, my mum would surely flog me for being here in the first place."

After what seemed like an eternity, they could finally see the main road. Suddenly the bus appeared and they all started to yell in hopes of attracting the attention of the driver. Adrian's anxiety was rekindled by the thought of being left behind. His stomach felt as though someone lit a yard fire in it but to his relief, the bus stopped and the conductor called to them to hurry.

Adrian had a déjà vu experience, where he felt as though he was still on the worn driveway of the school, trying not to be consumed by a stampede of his peers. The bag on his back felt just as heavy as before, as he ran towards the waiting bus, which seemed to glisten more brilliantly than before. This time the struggle was more intense. The driver was impatient and wanted to leave in case the policeman should pass again. No one wanted to be left and Adrian didn't fare too well this time. His frail frame was tossed to and fro, but not in the direction of the door. He wound up being the last to board and the driver didn't wait until he was fully inside before moving off.

Pulling himself fully into the moving bus, Adrian

breathed a sigh of relief, but things were not destined to improve just yet. Another bus came down the road and signalled Adrian's driver to stop. Adrian listened in bewilderment as the hailing driver warned that there was a policeman on the road ahead.

"I'm finished," thought Adrian, "we have to pass that road to get to town."

He started thinking about the distance to town on foot, but to his surprise, the driver suddenly careened the bus through a road Adrian had never even noticed. The driver increased speed, seemingly oblivious to the fact that the road had significantly decreased in size. Adrian didn't care that the road was not suited to their speed. He could smell the foulness of his peers with the same intensity he smelled himself, but it no longer mattered. He was prepared to endure the odours of a thousand armpits, but he could not fathom being evicted from the bus again. He had no clue where he was but he had faith that the bus would wind up in town, and hope that he would still be on it. Suddenly, the bus swung out of a minor road, onto a major road and Adrian recognised where he was. He was back on the correct bus route but closer to town.

"I'm going to make it," he thought, but then he heard the familiar sound of a siren.

This time the children responded differently. Though the bus was still overloaded, there were less of them and they could more easily manoeuvre. Adrian watched in amazement as tall fourth and fifth-formers contorted themselves under seats, asking the occupants of those seats to conceal them with their bags.

"I can't be put out," thought Adrian, "if they can hide then so can I."

He franticly looked around for a hiding place. He knew he didn't have much time as the policeman had already dismounted his bike and was walking towards the bus. The driver opened the door, its halves folding together and resting behind a single seat on the other side of the driver.

"I'm not going through that door until I reach town," Adrian thought to himself.

The officer boarded the bus and demanded to have only seven people standing. He was significantly bigger than the previous officer. His face was like a hardcourt and his eyes were cold. The unfortunate children who were unable to find hiding places were expelled from the bus. The policeman then turned his attention to the driver, who reached his hand backward to give the officer his credentials. He was reported for deviating from the prescribed route and the conductor was reported for overloading, again. The driver, now agitated, started off again. With the officer out of sight, the children who were under the seats emerged from their hiding places. As they reintegrated themselves into the standing crew, the driver closed the door. As the two hinged segments became straight, Adrian's figure was revealed. He had thrown his bag on the engine and squeezed himself between the folded door and the front passenger seat.

"I have to try that one next time, lil man," shouted a fourth-former to Adrian.

He was relieved to have gotten away with his stunt

and elated at the accolade. It was better to be known as 'the little man who tricked the police' than 'the freaky little man'.

The portion of the trip which followed brought a measure of tranquillity to Adrian. The traffic on the road prohibited the driver from perpetrating further recklessness. That is not to say that this portion of the journey was devoid of unwanted experiences, however. As the bus got closer to town, a number of the children disembarked at some of the bus stops along the way. Adrian thought this was a good thing, because then the load would be lessened and they wouldn't get any further police reports. At one of the stops, a particular girl disembarked.

"I know her," Adrian thought, "she lives in my street, but why is she getting off the bus here?"

He eventually concluded that she had to meet someone in the vicinity but he still wondered if there was another reason. He was, after all, new to this "culture", and could take nothing for granted.

As the journey continued, the bus stopped at a bus stop, and Adrian realised that no one had requested the stop. He peeped through the door as it opened, his jaw dropping as he saw what was happening. There was a multitude of children at the bus stop rushing towards the open door.

"What's happening?" Adrian queried inwardly.

The uniforms he could distinguish were from schools in the town vicinity. Therefore, these children had no need to take a bus into town, and furthermore, they would have had to walk out of town in order to get to this particular bus stop.

Adrian was puzzled but he did not have time to analyse the source of his puzzlement. Suddenly, the conductor tugged his arm.

"Lil man, step off the bus, you're getting out in town," he said.

Adrian was confused and frightened, but he said nothing as he saw others being subjected to the same treatment. Standing outside the bus with many of his peers, he watched the new crowd flood the door. To Adrian, they resembled ants descending upon a sweet treat; he didn't care to count them.

"Where will we go after this?" Adrian pondered, trying to subdue the anxious burning which had crept into his stomach.

"There will be no room for us when the ants get through."

The new crowd got into the bus fairly quickly and then the conductor told Adrian and the other displaced children to re-board.

"Where are we supposed to go?" thought Adrian, "I can't see anything but people beyond the steps."

The conductor started tugging children and shoving them into place on the steps. Adrian was left till last and shoved onto the last available step, which he shared with the conductor.

As the bus moved off the spot, Adrian wasn't sure whether to be grateful or dismayed. He was still, technically, in the bus, but only his fingers and toes had this privilege. His toes were on the step and his hands struggled to get a grip on the corrugated metal which lined the doorway. There were people in front of him, and this forced him to curve the rest of his body outward, so that his back and posterior hung through the door. Adrian was concerned that the part of him which was on the exterior of the vehicle would connect with a wall, fence or tree as the bus sped along. At least the wind was cooling his sweaty form, and if his back should collide with something, so would the conductor's.

As the bus neared the city, Adrian was greeted with an unbelievable sight; there was another multitude of children at an upcoming bus stop and they were signalling the bus to stop. Adrian's jaw dropped in disbelief—not at the number of children for there had been more at the previous stop, but at the fact that the driver was stopping.

"Where are you planning to put those children?" Adrian asked the conductor, expressing his thoughts audibly for the first time during the journey.

The conductor laughed heartily and replied, "Watch and learn, lil man, watch and learn."

Adrian watched but he did not learn. The conductor commanded the passengers to 'make themselves small', and there was suddenly more room available to Adrian. He was then able to make it to the top of the steps, unsure how the other passengers had accomplished the feat, but uncaring. At least he was no longer on the bottom step. The conductor declared that more space had to be created and commanded girls to sit on boys. More space quickly became available and Adrian felt like slapping himself.

"Good thing I lost my seat," he thought, picturing the outcome of a girl sitting on his lap.

"Boy," he thought, "if my mother ever found out she would dismantle me on the spot—for sure!"

His thoughts were interrupted by the sudden surge of the new passengers into the bus. Adrian felt like clay in a potter's hands, being compressed and contorted with no power to retaliate.

Soon the bus stop was cleared and the bus moved off. Adrian weighed in his mind which circumstance was more favourable—being partially outside the bus, or being compressed in this massive, smelly agglutination. The odour had intensified tenfold, and Adrian could visualise the armpits, waistlines and scalps which he smelled. He could also make out what some of the children had for lunch, as they spoke to each other around him. At least they were soon in town; they would soon be entering the bus yard and it would all be over.

Finally, after what felt like hours to Adrian, the bus approached the bus yard. Adrian started to get excited at the prospect of breathing fresh air again, but his excitement soon turned to wonderment, as the driver brought the bus to a dead stop instead of turning into the yard.

"What now?" he wondered.

The children soon answered that question, as they started to hit the sides of the bus in ecstatic anticipation of what was to come. It was evident that further recklessness was about to transpire.

An older girl shouted to the driver, "You know you

have to give us something proper."

The driver seemed to respond by revving the engine. Then the bus scratched off the mark and turned the first bend to enter the bus yard. The entire bus tilted on the right side.

The children raised a chorus, "Shakes, shakes, shakes for goodness sake!"

The driver straightened up and then took the second bend, tilting the vehicle even lower than before. A girl pushed her hand out the window and shouted with great excitement.

"I can almost touch the pavement!"

"Lord, please bring this bus back to its original position," Adrian prayed, fearful of being dismembered this close to his freedom.

His anxiety shot through the ceiling; he was surer of disaster at this moment than at any other during the trip. Amidst the cheering around him he could hear screams—some from outside and some from his own peers. Adrian regretted ever boarding this 'turbulent' bus. The popularity and acceptance which he craved now seemed insignificant. He was prepared to be unpopular; he now had an intense appreciation of life, regardless of status.

His prayer was answered and the bus returned to an upright position and jerked to a halt. Adrian experienced relief in greater magnitude than ever before in his life; it superseded the passing of a difficult exam or the emptying of a full bladder. He felt like a criminal on death row who had just been pardoned. However, Adrian was not allowed to savour this relief for too long.

Back in the real world, the cheering and chanting had increased drastically. Adrian peeped outside and made a startling realisation; the extra cheering and chanting was not coming from inside the bus, but from swarms of children outside. He then received further revelation; this time it scared him greatly. The children outside were ready to inundate the bus and they weren't planning to wait until the current passengers vacated. What ensued next was a horrific tug o' war.

Both the embarking and disembarking passengers struggled to get through the door, squeezing and crushing whoever was between them. Adrian managed to retrieve his bag from the engine but was caught in the crossfire. People were jumping through windows, the driver was tossing bags through the front window and Adrian lost all sense of direction and orientation. He felt like a puppet on several strings, unable to control the motion of his person. He was assaulted from all angles; his feet were mashed, his stomach was elbowed and he was even hit in the top of his head. A realisation then hit him in the midst of all the confusion; the girl who had gotten off the bus before it reached the yard probably knew that this would happen. He also realised that the last set of children to board the bus where actually trying to get home from town. They had walked out of town to board the bus before the inevitable madness of the bus yard rush. Eventually he made it out of the bus, through no action of his own, but he was still in the thick of the crowd of embarking children. He pushed his way through the masses of sweat-soaked flesh until finally he penetrated the mass and stepped into fresh air.

Adrian closed his eyes and breathed a deep breath of air, relieved that the ordeal was over and resolute never to repeat it. He opened his eyes, about to look for the bus home, and was greeted by a sight more dreadful than anything he had experienced all afternoon. His eyes fell in perfect contact with those of a big, brown, cruel-looking woman.

Adrian could only stammer, "F-f-f-ancy m-m-meeting y-y-you here, Mum."

THE HEIST

The morning breeze blew a solitary leaf from a towering tree, down into Adrian's face as he walked briskly into the school yard. Adrian barely noticed the leaf. The feeling of determination he felt was overshadowing everything else as he approached his unsuspecting targets—a group of his peers relaxing on benches under a tree. As he approached them, he slowed his pace, attempting to appear as relaxed as possible. They never suspected the furnace of anticipation and apprehension which roared inside of his stomach as he reached into his pocket. Adrian sat on a vacant bench next to his peers, completely unnoticed, but that was all about to change. His hand slowly exited his pocket, revealing the object of his salvation, the object that would finally empower him to make his mark—a handheld portable gaming console.

The children on the surrounding benches soon heard the sounds emanating from the gaming console as Adrian proceeded to load up a game and play it. It didn't take long before an audience gathered around Adrian's bench, gawking at the device.

"What the bird!" cried one boy. "That's a Gladiator 64?"

"That just released. How you got that already?" asked another. "That must cost an arm and a leg."

Adrian stifled the smile that was jostling to emerge, as he calmly said, "I have my connections."

Adrian remained outwardly calm as he continued to play but he was inwardly tingling with excitement, as the crowd grew larger. He didn't know which students had gathered, but it didn't matter. He could hear the voices of newcomers.

"Let me see. Let me see!"

This intensified his excitement. His plan was working, validating all of the time spent devising and executing it. The risks taken were all worth it; his journey to popularity had begun.

Suddenly, the gaming console was ripped from Adrian's hands. His head sprung up, surveying the crowd to see who had taken his console. His survey quickly revealed the console within the grip of two large, dark hands. Adrian adjusted his gaze upward to see the face with which these hands were associated. There was no mistaking that tarred, pink-eyed, flat face with a hippopotamus nose and hair like unkempt shrubbery. It was Ricardo, a fifth-former who was not to be messed with. He had never lost a fight, from first form till now and Adrian wasn't about to be added to his list of triumphs. On the contrary—Adrian saw this as an opportunity, springing up to show Ricardo the features of the device. Adrian was filled with a dichotomy of emotions. On the one hand, he was excited to be having discourse with a fifth-former of Ricardo's repute. On the other hand, he couldn't shake the uneasy feeling of apprehension that arose from the thought of his game in the control of a bully.

"What if he doesn't give it back?" he thought.

"I can't report it stolen because it's against the rules to have it in the first place."

The apprehension soon conquered the hopefulness. Adrian's heartrate increased drastically; he could feel his heart beating in his chest and he felt as though he couldn't keep up with his breathing.

Adrian's heartrate suddenly peaked with the piercing sound of the school's bell. It was time for assembly and the moment of truth for Adrian. Would Ricardo give him back the game? He would know in a matter of seconds, as the crowd began to steadily disperse, letting in the light which was previously blocked by the congregation. Adrian could feel the space around him becoming lighter and brighter, daring him to hope for a favourable outcome. Ricardo was still engrossed in the game, as if oblivious to the bell. Suddenly, Adrian realised a slight darkening of his immediate space as a new shadow overcame him. He looked back to see the principal, Wilberforce Harding, sternly staring at them. Adrian stood frozen, still processing the sight of this tall, slender, clear skinned man, with an Adam's apple the size of a small goitre, and a hairline receding into oblivion. He didn't breathe, nor did he blink, and he seemed physically incapable of moving. He watched helplessly as Principal Harding held his weathered palm out, which was promptly covered up with the gaming console Ricardo willingly surrendered to him.

"Now get to assembly before I flog you both!" Principal Harding said, sternly.

The boys dispersed. Adrian began to walk towards the assembly hall, passing under a long trellis and mounting the steps leading to the hall entrance, but it was as though someone else was walking for him. Adrian felt numb, and the entire experience felt unreal, as though he were watching a dream unfold, but the dream didn't end. As he entered the hall, he began to come to terms with the fact that this was reality. Throughout the morning, Adrian was preoccupied with despair and regret. He heard nothing that was said at assembly. One by one, his teachers entered the classroom and executed their lesson plans but Adrian couldn't focus. He kept reliving the events of that morning.

Earlier that morning as he sat at the dining table eating his cereal and drinking his hot chocolate, he had patiently waited for his mother to leave home for work, as usual.

"Did you press your clothes?" she asked.

"Yes, Mum," Adrian replied.

"Did you polish your shoes?"

"Yes, Mum," he replied, growing slightly annoyed with each new question.

"Do you have your lunch money?"

"Yes, Mum. I have everything covered," cried Adrian, "please, I don't want you to get to work late worrying about me."

"Fine. I'll leave you to it," she said, after staring at him for a bit.

"Sometimes I forget how much you've grown up."

Adrian watched quietly as she grabbed her hand bag and her keys, walked away through the living room and left the house.

The living room, dining room and kitchen were one physical space with imaginary lines dividing them, and a partition to the left, separating two bedrooms and a bathroom from the shared space.

That morning, after his mother had left the house, Adrian sat at the dining table, facing the living room and staring directly ahead at the front door and the clock directly above it. He waited exactly five minutes to ensure his mother hadn't forgotten anything at home, and then he made his move. Moving quickly, he removed the chairs from around the table, and he removed the vase that served as a centrepiece, along with his breakfast wares. He then pulled the table next to the partition and positioned one of the dining chairs next to it. He secured a foot pouffe from the living room and lifted it into place on top of the table, next to the partition. Then, carefully, he climbed onto the chair, then from the chair to the table, then from the table to the pouffe, giving him the height needed to pull his body over the partition and into his mother's locked room, landing on the bed.

The room was small and cramped. There wasn't much furniture—just a queen-sized bed and a chest of drawers, reducing his search variables drastically. After a quick peek under the bed, he then began to systematically investigate each drawer in the chest, until he found his prize in the third drawer—the Gladiator 64 portable gaming console, hidden in a brown plastic bag. His mother had confiscated it, fearing that he would take it to school, but that morning, he had it in his grasp and there was nothing and no one to stop him from doing just that.

Two hours later, in hindsight, it didn't seem like such a good idea after all. The triumph of finding the console had faded. The triumph of attracting a crowd of his peers had faded. All that remained was the dread of his mother discovering what he had done, and the subsequent laceration of his posterior as a result. That fear crippled him for the entire morning, but by the time the lunch bell rang, his sense of logic began to resurface amidst the fear. He didn't get to that point by wallowing in emotion; it was decisive, calculated actions that got the console out of his mother's custody, and it was decisive, calculated actions that would get it out of the principal's custody.

Adrian exited the classroom following the bell and stood in a dingy corridor with rails leading to a set of stairs to access the hardcourt below. As the other students filed through the door, he singled out three of them, whom he pulled to the side.

Alex was short, chubby and dark, with fat cheeks and a flat nose the most noteworthy embellishments on a wide face.

Jay was clear, average height and slim. His slender nose had a small hump in the middle of its bridge, like the back of a baby camel.

Ty was also average height but a little thicker than Jay, with a nose like an arrow. His complexion was sandwiched somewhere between that of Alex and Jay.

"I'm hungry, this better be good!" Alex cried, as he folded his arms.

Adrian relayed the events of that fateful morning to them.

"Why are we now hearing about this?" cried Ty.

"It got confiscated before I could get to you," replied Adrian.

"Please …" started Alex, "you weren't bringing the game to us, you were trying to impress people."

"I, I, I was just trying to widen our small circle," replied Adrian with a stammer and a fake smile.

"I had you in thoughts the whole time, and now, I need your help."

Jay looked at him with a sceptical look.

"How?" he asked, folding his arms.

"I need a diversion," started Adrian, as he leaned casually against the railing, "a couple of them, actually; I'm going to break into the principal's office."

The other three boys stared at Adrian wide-eyed.

"Are you mad?" Alex cried in a loud voice.

"Not at all," started Adrian, "I just need to get the principal out of the office long enough that I can sneak past the receptionist."

The boys stared at Adrian with their arms folded.

"The only sure way to do that is to start a fight!" cried Ty.

"Exactly!" replied Adrian, with wide eyes.

Alex responded to him in a slow manner, as if for

him to understand.

"A-dri-an, we … will … be … flogged."

Adrian replied in the same manner, "A-lex, you … will … be … paid."

Alex's eyes lit up.

"Well, that's different. Why didn't you say so?" he started, unfolding his arms.

"Who do I hit? When do I hit them?"

Ty's hand flew up.

"I'm in."

Jay looked sternly at Adrian and said, "No way; you know I hate getting into trouble."

Adrian assured Jay that he had another job for him to do, and a plan was set in motion.

Alex and Ty entered the crowded canteen area and joined one of the queues leading to the serving windows.

Alex looked back at Ty and asked, "Big man, you just brush me?"

Ty replied, "The canteen's full, you can't expect not to be touched."

Alex turned his stocky body completely around to face Ty.

"Say sorry!"

Ty indifferently replied, "Never!"

Alex folded his fist.

"Very well."

He then hit Ty alongside his head with force, knocking him backward and downward. Ty flew up and returned the blow as the children went wild in a chant.

"Fight, fight, fight!"

No one seemed to be interested in lunch anymore. Every nook and cranny of the school delivered up their students, who all descended on the canteen to witness the spectacle.

Not everyone was running towards the fight, though. Adrian and Jay were hiding behind a hedge, watching the main office. Principal Harding soon emerged and started briskly walking towards the scene of the commotion, as Adrian had anticipated. As soon as the principal passed the hedge, Adrian and Jay sprung from behind it, and ran to the office. Jay burst through the office door in a frenzy.

"Please, Ma'am, help me. I can't find my inhaler," he started.

"Can I please call my mother to make sure I didn't leave it at home?"

The receptionist sprang up from her seat to look over the counter, which was taller than the desktop behind it. As her attention was fixed on Jay, Adrian was crawling past the desk, which was enclosed at the side with a desk-high partition and a small hinged door. He cleared the reception area and quietly entered the hallway behind the reception. This hallway had only two doors—the principal's office and the sick bay. Adrian quickly but quietly entered the principal's office, which was big and spacious, with a big desk in the middle, a trophy display cabinet on the wall facing the desk and a low ceiling. There was a wall of windows facing the school compound but venetian blinds were in place and closed. Adrian was elated that his plan was working beautifully but he knew he had to be quick. His heart started to pound as he started going through the drawers on either side of the desk. This was not like earlier that morning, when his mother had left for work; the principal was not far away and he had to find the game and get out of there before the principal finished flogging his friends, and before Jay's distraction expired. Adrian found the game in the fifth drawer searched, retrieved it, closed the drawer promptly and dashed for the door. Just then, he heard footsteps coming down the hallway and knew he had to think fast. He wasn't about to be caught in that compromising position so he quickly repositioned himself to the only hiding place in the entire office—underneath the desk.

As the principal entered the room, Adrian was crouched underneath the desk in the left corner. All he could see was the seat of the principal's chair and the wall behind the chair. He could, however, hear all that was transpiring. The principal had decided to flog the boys in his office instead of on the spot.

"You know we have a zero-tolerance policy on fighting," boomed the principal's voice.

Adrian knew what was coming next. His heart was thumping like a bass speaker in a reggae song. He was afraid to even breathe. He couldn't tell if the sudden chill he felt was the air conditioning or a bad premonition of things to come. He heard the whoosh of the belt as it cut through the air and he flinched as he heard it hit its target. He could hear scuffling as his friends repositioned their bodies with every lash, each one sounding more dreadful than the last. Then came the sound of whimpering, piercing Adrian's still throbbing heart to its core. This operation had cost him all of his lunch money, but now, hearing first-hand what it had cost his friends, the hunger he felt seemed a worthy recompense for what he had put them through. To Adrian's relief, the flogging came to an abrupt end, and the boys scampered out of the office.

That relief, however, was soon replaced by a new dread, as the principal took his place at the desk. His right foot rested just next to Adrian, who tried to make himself as small as possible, so as not to be accidentally kicked and discovered. A moment before, Adrian didn't think his heart could beat any faster, but now, somehow, it was, and he couldn't slow it down. As if his predicament wasn't bad enough, the principal slid his feet out of his shoes. The scent that emanated from his socks was nothing short of repugnant. It smelled like a carpet that had been wet and left damp for three months. Adrian started to feel sick, wondering what died and decayed between Principal Harding's toes, but he couldn't risk reacting and being discovered. Suddenly, there was a piercing sound followed by an odour rivalling the socks. Principal Harding had broken wind, and he wasn't finished. There was a rapid succession of flatulent emissions, filling Adrian's air supply with the scent of two landfills amalgamated. This, together with the smell of the socks brought water to Adrian's eyes. It was more than he could bear and he had visions of himself passing out from the combined scent.

Just then, as if by some divine intervention, there was a knock at the principal's door and the receptionist called him away to speak to a parent in the reception area. Principal Harding slipped his shoes back on and exited the room, giving Adrian a brief window of escape—but how? The principal was mere metres away in the reception area. There was no way he was going to get out the way he came in and this assessment sent Adrian into a panic.

"What can I do?" he thought to himself.

"Lifting the venetian blinds and window will be too noisy," he thought, "and I won't be able to bring them down again from outside."

There was also the fact that he could easily be seen exiting by the windows, as they faced the school compound. Time was running out, neither the door nor window was an option, and those were the only two openings in the room.

"I'm finished," he thought, "there's nothing I can do.

"I'd have to go through the ceiling."

Then it hit him—he could go through the ceiling. It was low enough to reach if he stood on the desk and there was a manhole conveniently in reach. Adrian wasted no time; he put the game in his pocket, stood on the desk, pushed the manhole cover up and out of place and then hoisted himself up through the hole in the ceiling. His upper body strength, or lack thereof, should have made this a challenging feat, but the adrenaline seemed to imbue him with super powers. By the time he heard the principal's footsteps approaching the office, he was already in the ceiling and returning the cover to its rightful position.

Adrian began his journey through the ceiling. It was dark, dusty and cramped, but it was a more favourable accommodation than under the desk. He relied on the game to provide light for him to navigate. Bathrooms were located to the back of the office block, and Adrian knew there was a manhole in the boys' bathroom, just over the changing benches. He averaged the distance and direction, careful to travel on the strong wooden beams, moving as slowly and as lightly as he could, so as not to make a sound. Finally, he reached his destination. The bell rang, signaling lunch break would soon end, just as he was removing the manhole cover. Anxious to get back to his class and secure the game in his backpack, Adrian promptly jumped down through the hole. He landed in a bathroom stall, in front of a toilet. His eyes met with the eyes of a girl, sitting on the toilet! He had miscalculated, exiting in the girls' bathroom instead. The poor, startled girl began to scream to the top of her lungs, as Adrian dashed from the stall and out of the bathroom, leaving a wake of screaming behind him. He did not look back, nor did he stop running until he reached the classroom.

Adrian sat at his desk, struggling to catch his breath. His heart was pounding, but so was his head. Dropping into the girl's stall had given him an instant headache. His friends gathered around him.

"Never again!" cried Alex.

"You got the game?" asked Jay.

"I couldn't hold out any longer. How'd you get out?"

Adrian heard the questions but was unable to answer. All the air seemed to have evacuated his lungs. He eventually caught his breath and filled them in just as the last lunch bell rang. Going into the next period he felt relaxed and relieved. He had been through an ordeal, but he made it. He had the game and the principal had no idea that it was his, since it had been confiscated from Ricardo. Yes, he had the incident in the girls' bathroom, but he had never seen the girl on the toilet before that day, so he was pretty confident she didn't know him. As for the other girls in the bathroom, he had exited with such haste that he was certain no one knew who he was. He had actually succeeded— or had he?

Halfway into the period after lunch, Adrian happened to look through the window to the corridor. He could see the principal and the girl from the bathroom stall going from classroom to classroom. He started to panic inside.

"What am I going to do?" he thought.

"She's going to single me out to the principal for sure."

Just then, the frail, greying teacher noticed Adrian fidgeting restlessly.

"Adrian," she shouted, "focus!"

Adrian's brain was in overdrive. He hadn't come this far to get into trouble now.

"I'm sorry, Ma'am," he started.

"I'm distracted because I really need to use the bathroom, but I didn't want to ask for an excuse because I know I should have gone during lunch."

The teacher was noticeably annoyed, but Adrian

was hoping she would be compassionate towards his plight since he had acknowledged his fault in the matter.

"Alright," she said, "you may go."

Adrian sprang up, exclaiming, "Thank you so much, Ma'am!"

He tried to make her think he was grateful for the opportunity to relieve himself but in actuality, he was grateful for the opportunity to be absent when the principal reached that class. He dashed to the bathroom, taking a route that kept him out of the principal's sight.

When Adrian reached the bathroom, he found a congregation of mostly older boys who had skipped class to gamble. He didn't want any loose ends—people that could identity or place him in a particular location. He dashed into one of the stalls as quickly and inconspicuously as possible. The stall was cramped, with an abundance of graffiti on the walls, most of which said or represented things Adrian would never dare repeat. He wasn't in the stall for two minutes when he heard the voice of a teacher booming.

"All of you, come with me to the principal's office!"

Adrian froze. He couldn't believe this was happening.

"You in the stall," cried the teacher, "come out at once!"

Adrian's heart started to pound—a sensation he was starting to get accustomed to. He knew he had to think of something fast—another thing he was starting to get accustomed to. He quickly dropped his pants, grabbed the roll of toilet paper from on top of the toilet tank and opened the stall door, revealing himself to the teacher—and the other boys.

"Sir," he started, with his shirttail hanging down to his thighs, "I'm not gambling with them. I really had to go."

That sight and explanation resulted in a chorus of laughter from the boys.

Later that evening, Adrian stood in his mother's bedroom, with the third drawer of her chest of drawers open. As he was about to return the game to its expected position, he recounted all the events of the day. What started out as a plan to gain popularity turned out to be a series of unfortunate events, culminating in humiliation. By the time the last bell rang the entire school had been informed that Adrian was caught defecating at school. The only silver lining to all the dark clouds was the fact that his mother would never find out about it. He promptly returned the game to the black plastic bag and closed the drawer. The partition he had climbed over was boxed on that side, so he was able to climb up on the wooden boxing and hoist himself over the top. It was soon time for his mother to return home, so he wasted no time in returning the table, chairs, pouffe and even the vase to their rightful places in the house. Everything was as it was before his mother left home, and Adrian sat at the dining table and started to do his homework.

His mother came home at the expected time, visibly tired, and disappeared into her room to undress and prepare for a shower. Adrian knew he had returned everything as it was, and for the first time in about eight hours, he was at total peace. Suddenly, he heard his mother's voice booming from the bedroom.

"You think I was born yesterday, boy?"

"I left this game in a brown plastic bag. Bring the belt!"

NEW CLOTHES

It was the first day of the new school term and Adrian was on his way to the city after a rainy first day. As he sat in the back seat of the bus, he reflected on how he had managed to keep himself clean during the day. He had a completely new school uniform, from shirt to shoes, and his mother would go ballistic if he came home with any part of it soiled. It had been raining the entire day and he had resisted the temptation to play football with his friends at recess. He had even eaten his lunch in an isolated area to avoid accidents.

As the bus approached the hospital on the outskirts of the city, Adrian noticed some of the other students looking back. He turned to look through the back windshield to see the popular bus coming behind them. The other bus was gaining on them as it swerved recklessly at a high rate of speed, rocking from side to side in every bend. Adrian looked on in relief that he wasn't in that bus, as he had experienced such recklessness first-hand and did not find it as exciting as the popular children did. Furthermore, it had been raining heavily the entire day, and though the rains had subsided, Adrian was sure the roads weren't conducive to that kind of recklessness.

"Those stupid children are probably encouraging the driver to do those reckless stunts," he thought to himself, but he couldn't be overly bothered.

"If they want to get themselves killed, that is a matter for them," he thought, as he indifferently turned around to face forward and focus on his own ride.

Suddenly, he heard loud gasps followed by screams. Before he could investigate the source or cause of these outbursts, there was a loud bang and Adrian felt his body being thrown forward into the centre aisle, the bang still echoing in his ears. The bus came to a halt and before long, the children started to disembark. Adrian felt a hand tugging on his arm, pulling him to stand up. It was his friend Alex, a short, dark, chubby boy with fat cheeks and a nose as flat as a two-by-four.

"You alright?" asked Alex.

"We got hit by *Turbulence*."

Adrian looked at Alex with a puzzled expression.

"What do you mean by that," asked Adrian, "you think this is a plane, Big Man?"

Alex stared at him with an exasperated look on his face as he replied.

"The bus that was driving behind us is called *Turbulence* and that is what hit us."

Adrian felt stupid and tried to cover up his blunder.

"Oh, I understand now.

"I was a little disoriented from the jolt."

Alex looked at him with a sceptical look.

"Sure," he said, "I think we should get out of here. It'll be a while before the police respond."

"The children are looking to walk into town."

The boys filed out of the bus and gathered with the other students, just outside the hospital, to visually assess the situation before starting their journey into town. By that time there was a large crowd gathered, comprising of children from both buses as well as curious passersby. They were joined by their friends, Jay and Ty, who were also on the bus with them.

Jay was a clear, slim boy of average height with a bony humped nose. Ty was brown and of similar build to Jay, just a little thicker with a pointed nose.

As they tried to figure out how the accident occurred, Adrian was approached by a dark girl of average height who was slim but quite shapely. Her hair was immobilised by an overly generous helping of hair gel and her uniform clung to her body like the inflated cuff of a blood pressure gauge.

"You were on the bus in the front, right?" she asked.

Adrian could only nod, still processing the sight of this African goddess. He had seen her around the school and even had an experience with her once on the bus, but this was the first opportunity he had ever gotten to actually speak to her—if only he could get the words out.

"I think the brakes on *Turbulence* failed, or got too hot, or something.

"Everybody alright over there?" she asked.

Now was Adrian's big moment; anxiety burned within his stomach and he could feel his chest becoming tight as he forced the words out.

"Y-y-y-yes, please," said Adrian, fidgeting with the material in his pants pocket, "j-just a little jolt but everyone seems to be fine."

Alex, Jay and Ty just stared at Adrian. His infatuation was obvious.

"You just say 'yes, please'?" asked the girl with a chuckle.

"That's so cute. You always this polite, and so neat and clean?"

Adrian tried to respond but all he could do was blush.

Smiling widely, the girl looked at Adrian and his friends and said, "Come, we' going to cross the canal and head into the bus yard.

"We know how to get across, even when it rains."

Adrian replied, "Right behind you."

As the girl walked off, carrying a group of popular children behind her, Adrian's friends stared at him shaking their heads.

"What?" cried Adrian.

"First, you are pathetic," said Alex, gesturing with his hands.

"She thinks I'm cute," replied Adrian, promptly but calmly.

"Second, you are mad," Alex continued, pointing in the direction of the canal.

"We've crossed the canal before …"

"Under normal conditions but it's been raining the whole day."

Ty chimed in, "He's right, the water's going to overflow the banks.

"We should go through the public park."

"That will take longer and the clouds are getting darker," started Adrian, "we need the quickest route to the bus yard and she knows how to get across."

Adrian dashed off behind the popular crowd, as the majority of the children veered to the right, to go through the public park. Alex, Jay and Ty hesitated, briefly consulting among themselves. Ty started to follow Adrian. Jay and Alex looked at each other and then joined him. The decision had been made and they would soon learn whether or not it was a good one, as the walk to the canal was only about five minutes.

The canal was a dirty, mossy channel just over a metre wide and thirty centimetres deep. It was set in a descent of marshes, which stretched about five hundred and fifty metres, on a route which passed alongside the bus yard, until it flowed into a much wider channel in the middle of the city, leading to the sea. The children reached the marshlands at a point where there was a man-made path sloping down the descent, through the marshes and leading to the canal. Where the path met the canal, there was a plank stretched across the canal for persons to cross. However, on that occasion, due to the constant rain during the day, the water had risen above the canal walls, overflowing onto the banks and completely covering the plank. Adrian watched with great interest and admiration as his African goddess put one foot into the water where the plank should be, and felt around a little until she found it. Knowing where the plank was, she then proceeded to carefully walk across the canal, balancing on the unseen plank. While on top of the plank, the water didn't cover her entire shoe, and she made it to the other side without getting her socks wet. One by one, the other popular children crossed the canal in the same fashion, with those who had successfully crossed waiting and cheering on those to come. As the last of the popular children crossed, the group started to call to Adrian and his friends, cheering them on to cross.

The thought of being considered part of their group greatly appealed to Adrian. The thought of these popular children cheering for them appealed to him even more.

"I'm going for it," cried Alex, stepping to the edge of the water.

Once there, he paused, as if thinking to himself.

"What's the matter?" asked Adrian.

"This backpack is heavy," Alex replied, shaking himself a little to test the weight, "it could cause me to lose balance."

"Well, throw it across."

Taking Adrian's suggestion, Alex took off his backpack and threw it across the canal. With his bag safely on the other side, Alex then put his foot into the water where the others had put theirs, and quickly found the plank. He took the first step onto the plank and then attempted the second but midway in the second step, he started to lose balance, affected by the current of the swiftly flowing water in the canal. Alex quickly stepped back and returned to the bank behind him. After two more failed attempts, the children on the other side started to 'boo'.

Ty looked at Jay and said, "We can't let Alex ruin our moment to be cool."

They proceeded to cross the canal together, Ty in front and Jay following in his footsteps close behind. Ty was about to set foot on the other bank when Jay's foot landed on a piece of debris—either moss or bush that had become hooked around the plank—instead of the level plain of the plank. It was enough to throw off his balance and as he started falling, he grabbed Ty for support. This sudden and unexpected tug caused Ty to lose his balance as well. Both boys fell screaming into the dirty, mossy canal, water entering their mouths, noses and eyes. As the children laughed, Adrian included, Ty and Jay promptly pulled themselves out of the canal, covered in moss and unidentified filth and ran to the nearby hospital.

"I can't believe this," cried Adrian, "you're making us look like a bunch of nerds.

"It can't be that hard!"

Adrian stepped forward to cross, anxious to prove himself worthy of affiliation to the popular group of children. He successfully found the plank and made his first step. As he made the second step, feeling the pull of the current on his foot, he then started to think about what would happen if he fell in. Not only would he humiliate himself in front of the popular crowd, but his mother would destroy him if he soiled his clothes, or found out he had taken such a stupid risk. As he completed his second step and heard the cheers of the children, the risk didn't seem so stupid anymore, and he continued, carefully, until reaching the other side.

"Way to go," shouted his African goddess, "you're the man!"

Adrian beamed with triumph, partially in disbelief that he had made it; his past schemes for popularity had never gone according to plan but things seemed to be turning around.

Adrian may have crossed successfully but there was still the issue of reuniting Alex with his bag.

"Come on," cried one of the children, "my grandmother could get across."

Alex made another attempt to cross the canal, but aborted again before completing the second step. By that time the other children had given up on him and started to leave, remarking that he was a nerd.

"Adrian," he cried, "you can't leave me like this.

"At least throw my bag across so I can go through the park before the rain starts again."

After the reaction of the popular children, Adrian didn't feel like being associated with Alex in that moment, but reuniting him with his bag was the least he could do. Stepping to the edge of the water, he picked the bag up and threw it towards Alex, but he underestimated the weight of the bag, and it landed in the canal like a meteorite crashing in the desert, splashing up water and moss on both Alex and himself.

Alex cried out, "We always get the 'dirty end of the stick' in your schemes.

"You're lucky I can't get across there!"

He fished his bag out of the canal and turned to go the long way. Adrian was relieved that Alex couldn't reach him but children were now laughing at him and his shirt was stained by the moss. Suddenly, popularity didn't matter; he knew he had to get home before his mother to wash his shirt.

Adrian walked with the group, enduring the laughter until the topic changed. By the time they ascended the slope out of the marshes on the other side, the topic of conversation had changed. The topic in his mind, however, never changed; he was concerned about his mother. The accident and diversion across the canal had cost him some time but he knew he should have enough time to get home before his mother. The problem was that his mother worked in the city, and after a prior questionable decision on his part, she sometimes popped out of work to pass through the bus yard to spy on him. The group was now on the road to the bus yard which was about two hundred and fifty metres from the crossing point. The road was very deserted, with little activity; the only vehicles that used that road were the buses leaving the bus yard. To the left of the road was the continuing stretch of marshes they had just ascended out of, and to the right of the road were patches of grass and gravel. The group was on a sidewalk on the left side of the road and as they approached the bus yard, Adrian inserted himself into the thick of the group so as to avoid detection should his mother be spying. Upon reaching the bus yard, however, the children began to disperse, each looking to board their respective buses, or join queues for buses yet to come. As the crowd dispersed a voice came piercing through the rumble of bus engines and pedestrian chatter.

"Adrian!"

Adrian looked around to see a big, brown, cruel-looking woman, in a white and black, horizontally striped dress. It was his mother and she did not look pleased.

"First day of school, shoes dripping wet, shirt looking mossy!" she started shouting, as a crowd gathered, inclusive of Adrian's peers.

"How did you get that white shirt green?" she continued, "I'm going to dirty you with blows!"

Adrian looked around at the crowd that had gathered. People were taking out mobile phones, presumably to capture the incident. He couldn't allow himself to be chastised in such a public forum. He would never be allowed to live it down and it would retard the progress of his popularity in the school. Then his eyes met with those of his African goddess, and he knew what he had to do—run like the wind.

Phones raised in the air as Adrian's mother took off behind him. With Adrian's white shirt and brown pants, and his mother's stripes, it resembled a well-fed zebra chasing a malnourished gazelle. As Adrian ran towards another canal crossing to exit the bus yard, he looked back in disbelief at the speed his mother was achieving. The part of the canal he was approaching was not as wide as the one he had crossed previously, and he was able to leap across the entire width of the waterway without issue. Landing on the other side and maintaining momentum, he gazed back to see his mother slipping on a piece of moss and sliding, screaming, straight into the canal. Adrian halted in horror, coming to terms with what had just happened to his mother—and what it meant for him. By this time, she was frantically trying to pull herself out of the canal, but the walls of the channel were mossy and her hands kept slipping.

"Oh my gosh, what should I do?" Adrian thought to himself.

"If I try to help her out, she will destroy me on the spot, if she doesn't pull me in with her first but if I don't, she will be mad as a hatter when she gets home."

As Adrian debated with himself, some men began helping her out of the canal, as curious passersby captured with their phones. Adrian wasn't waiting around to be captured on camera, and he took off running again, his mother quickly re-engaging pursuit.

"She seems more determined than ever," Adrian thought to himself, "she will tear me to shreds."

Adrian came to a set of traffic lights which were taking forever to change, causing him to look back to the sight of his mother in blistering pursuit. Her shoes made swishing noises as she ran, her dress was soiled with miscellaneous manners of filth and moss was tangled in her hair. Adrian had never seen his mother as angry as she looked now, and he wasn't about to investigate the boundaries of this new anger in such a public place. The traffic lights were still uncooperative with his cause, so he dashed into a nearby public market and into the men's bathroom.

The bathroom was awful, inundated with the scent of ammonia. All the tiles on the floor were wet, and that, coupled with the smell of ammonia, led Adrian to envision all of that floor-bound liquid as urine. Adrian heard a squishing noise and looked through the door to catch a glimpse of his mother running past the bathroom, going deeper into the market. As she ran, she left a wake of onlookers, visibly overtaken with curiosity and amusement. Adrian's concentration was suddenly broken by the sound of water hitting the ground. He ventured a little further into the bathroom to be disgusted by the sight of a man relieving himself on the floor, seemingly validating his earlier hypothesis—the tiles were inundated with urine. Adrian froze for a minute, processing the thought that his shoes were threading through the amalgamated urine of countless vagabonds and vagrants. His skin started to crawl, feeling as if the urine had somehow penetrated his shoes and contacted his feet. The man who was relieving himself concluded his deed and looked around to see Adrian in a daze.

"Peeping Tom!" he shouted.

"Who, me?" cried Adrian. "You've got it all wrong."

The man wasn't hearing it, as he proceeded to bellow.

"Security!"

Adrian wasn't waiting around to be apprehended by a guard. He turned and dashed for the bathroom exit, slipping on the wet tiles. As he fell backwards through the air it was like time slowed.

"I'm about to land in all this urine," he thought to himself, cringing in anticipation.

He hit the floor and slid forward through the door, cringing more with every passing second, for what seemed an eternity. The man from the bathroom continued to shout for security, and Adrian could see the guard coming in the distance.

There was no time to waste so he quickly snapped himself out of his state of cringing and jumped up off the floor. As he steadied himself to escape the market, he heard that familiar squishing sound, and looked behind him to see his mother quickly approaching. The zebra was at his rear, the urinator at his right, the guard at his left and the exit directly ahead. Adrian availed himself of the exit and dashed back to the traffic lights, which had just changed in his favour. Dashing across the road, his eyes fell on the closest building—a three-story department store.

"This is the perfect place to lose her," Adrian thought, and dashed into the store as his mother crossed the road behind him, her stripes blending with the zebra crossing on which she threaded.

Adrian dashed through the store, manoeuvring through the crowds. He was counting on the store being crowded and was sure of success. He could hear the squishing of his mother's shoes in the near distance so he knew she was still on his trail. He saw an elevator about to close and dashed into it, turning to stare his approaching predator in the face as the doors closed. Her eyes were red and he could see veins bulging in her neck as shoppers stared. This visual haunted him as the elevator went up and he was more determined than ever to lose her and get home before she could take out her anger on him in public. The elevator stopped and the doors opened to present the clothing department. Adrian dashed into the Men's Wear section.

"Thank God!" cried someone still in the elevator, but Adrian didn't care what discomfort he may have caused them.

He picked up a shirt from a rack which he proceeded to take to the changing rooms. There, he approached an attendant, a short, stout, clear-skinned woman with short curls.

"Excuse me, Ma'am," Adrian started, "I'd like to try this on please."

The woman looked at Adrian sternly and snatched the shirt.

"Looking and smelling like that?" she bellowed.

"Get lost!"

Adrian was bewildered. He had planned to hide in the changing room for a bit. Just then, he heard the sound of the elevator and looked around to see the second elevator opening to reveal ever widening black and white stripes; his mother had arrived. She spotted him and dashed through the Men's Wear section after him. Adrian dashed through the aisles of clothing in true gazelle fashion, zigging and zagging in his route in an attempt to throw his mother off his trail. He crossed out of the men's department and into the ladies' department, where a full-figured sale was in progress. There were various mannequins on display, clothed in a variety of outfits. Adrian could hear the squishing of his mother's shoes nearby, but a couple racks of clothing were blocking them from seeing each other. He knew he had to find a hiding place quickly as he scanned the mannequins which stood before him. One was wearing an Indian inspired outfit, another displayed an African inspired outfit, and still, another displayed a European inspired outfit. The mannequins were all full-figured but Adrian dashed behind the one with the African garb, as it was the widest of the three. He dared not peep from behind the mannequin as he heard the squish of his mother's shoes approaching; this was the moment of truth.

The swishing of the shoes came directly in front of the mannequins, and the sound stopped. Adrian held his breath and held perfectly still, his heart racing like a horse in a derby. The store was air conditioned but sweat started to drip from his face.

"She's on to me," he thought, "she knows I'm in this area. I'm finished."

Suddenly, the swishing resumed and continued into the distance. Adrian breathed a sigh of relief, but he dared not risk an exit as yet. After waiting about five minutes, he satisfied himself that the coast was clear as the squishing sound did not return. Adrian hurriedly but carefully exited his hiding place. With no zebra in sight, he made his way out of the store and set a course for the bus yard.

As Adrian made his way through the city and back to the bus yard, he had time to reflect on the events of the day.

"How do I manage to get myself in these situations?" he thought.

"I got through school with my clothes spotless and I just had to go crossing a dirty canal in my new clothes."

In retrospect, he was happy to have gained the acceptance of the popular children, however fleeting the moments may have been. However, he had to ask himself if it was worth it. As he neared the bus yard, he was calmed by the absence of his mother's swishing shoes but simultaneously anxious about what would happen when she eventually got home. As he entered the bus yard, he tried to envision what his mother would do. He had disappointed her many times but this was the first time his actions had resulted in direct misfortune for her. Adrian's bus was loading and he proceeded to board, conscious of the fact that he looked dirty and smelled like ammonia. This was a source of great humiliation as other passengers looked at him in the worst ways possible but it wasn't a deterrent; he had to get home. He made his way to the back of the bus and sat in the back seat between an Indian lady and an old man, holding his breath, waiting to see if either of them would confront him about his smell. As soon as he sat, the Indian lady grabbed his arm. Startled, he looked around to see what was happening as the lady removed her head garb to reveal her identity; it was his mother, in the same Indian inspired suit that was on sale in the department store.

She said in a loud voice, "You people like to put things on social media these days.

NEW CLOTHES

"Well, you're going to want to capture this!"

Coming next in the *Adrian* Series

Adrian at LAST

See the synopsis on the next page

Adrian at LAST

Barbados schoolboy, Adrian Manning is back at it again, still trying to attain popularity and struggling to survive the pitfalls associated with those attempts. Now fourteen years old, his newly honed football skills may finally be the key to securing popularity.

The road to reach acclaim is a dangerous one, but the destination brings its own perils with it, and to maintain that position threatens to be equally hazardous.

What happens when you finally get the thing you have been craving for so long? Does it live up to your high expectations? Is it worth the journey to get there? Is it worth the sacrifices to keep it?

Find the answers to these questions as Adrian goes from obscurity to fame, and everyone knows the name, Adrian—at last.

Redcore
PUBLISHING